"When did you get those bracelets?" Elizabeth asked her sister.

Jessica looked down at their bedroom floor. "I don't know," she whispered.

"How could you not know?" Elizabeth asked. She was puzzled. She looked over at the night table between their beds, and her mouth dropped open. "Jessica!" she gasped. "What happened to our money?"

"Ummm . . ." Jessica began. Her face was slowly turning red.

Elizabeth stared at her sister. She had worked so hard selling lemonade to help buy their teacher's wedding present. "Did you spend it? Did you buy those bracelets with our money?"

Instead of answering, Jessica burst into tears.

Bantam Skylark Books in the SWEET VALLEY KIDS series

SWEET VALLEY KIDS

ELIZABETH'S SUPER-SELLING LEMONADE

Written by
Molly Mia Stewart

Created by
FRANCINE PASCAL

Illustrated by
Ying-Hwa Hu

A BANTAM SKYLARK BOOK ®
NEW YORK · TORONTO · LONDON · SYDNEY · AUCKLAND

To Matthew Julian Weiss

RL 4, 008–012

ELIZABETH'S SUPER-SELLING LEMONADE
A Bantam Skylark Book / July 1990

Sweet Valley High® and Sweet Valley Twins and Friends®
are registered trademarks of Francine Pascal

Conceived by Francine Pascal

Produced by Daniel Weiss Associates, Inc.
33 West 17th Street
New York, NY 10011

Cover art by James Mathewuse

Skylark Books is a registered trademark of Bantam Books, a division
of Bantam Doubleday Dell Publishing Group, Inc. Registered in U.S.
Patent and Trademark Office and elsewhere.

ISBN 0-553-15807-4

Published simultaneously in the United States and Canada

Bantam Books are published by Bantam Books, a division of Bantam Doubleday
Dell Publishing Group, Inc. Its trademark, consisting of the words "Bantam
Books" and the portrayal of a rooster, is Registered in U.S. Patent and Trademark
Office and in other countries. Marca Registrada. Bantam Books, 1540 Broadway,
New York, New York 10036.

PRINTED IN THE UNITED STATES OF AMERICA

OPM 9 8 7 6 5

CHAPTER 1

Important Decisions

Elizabeth Wakefield was hanging upside down from the jungle gym at recess. It was a sunny Friday at Sweet Valley Elementary School. "Isn't it exciting that Mrs. Becker is getting married again?" she asked her twin sister, Jessica.

Mrs. Becker was the twins' teacher. Her first husband had died five years ago, and she had recently announced her engagement to Mr. Otis, a librarian at Sweet Valley Public Library.

"It is," Jessica said. "And I can't believe that we get to go to the wedding." Mrs.

Becker had invited the whole class to share her special day. Jessica flipped over the monkey bars and hung upside down next to Elizabeth. "Your shirt is coming down," she whispered.

Elizabeth held her green T-shirt in place and looked over at Jessica with a grin. Side by side, they looked like two upside-down peas in a pod. Both girls had blue-green eyes and long blond hair with bangs. They had many matching outfits, although Jessica always chose pink and yellow while Elizabeth liked blue and green. When they wore the same color outfits, no one in their second-grade class could tell them apart. They were the only identical twins at school.

Jessica and Elizabeth were identical on the outside, but they were very different on the inside. Each twin had her own likes and dislikes. Jessica liked playing with her dollhouse and passing notes in class. Her favorite subjects were lunch and recess! Elizabeth liked playing outdoor games, reading, and doing her homework.

Even though they were different, Elizabeth and Jessica were best friends. They shared a bedroom, they shared secrets, and they always split candy and treats right in half. Being identical twins was very special.

"Do you think we should get Mrs. Becker a present?" Elizabeth asked her sister.

"Are you talking about the wedding?" Lila Fowler asked, as she joined them on the jungle gym. She was Jessica's best friend after Elizabeth. "I know all about wedding presents," Lila said. "Microwave ovens or china dishes make perfect gifts."

Elizabeth swung her feet over the bar and landed on the sand. "I don't think we can get Mrs. Becker something like that," she said.

3

"Silverware is good, too," Lila went on in a know-it-all voice.

"That's too expensive," Jessica said. She shook her head and her ponytail swung from side to side.

Todd Wilkins and Winston Egbert were sitting on the top bar of the jungle gym. "Why do you want to get silverware?" Todd called.

"We want to buy Mrs. Becker a wedding present," Jessica told him.

Elizabeth frowned. "I was thinking about getting her some rainbow pencils for marking homework."

"You were?" Lila gasped. She laughed as if that were the silliest thing she had ever heard.

Jessica let her arms hang down. "I know. Let's ask the principal."

"Good idea!" Elizabeth said.

The principal of Sweet Valley Elementary School, Mrs. Armstrong, was standing next

5

to the slide, watching Jerry McAllister and Charlie Cashman. The two boys always got into trouble for going down headfirst.

Jessica jumped down next to Elizabeth.

"We're coming, too," Winston said.

"Who asked you?" Lila said in a bossy voice. "It wasn't *your* idea." Winston looked at Lila, crossed his eyes, and stuck out his tongue.

"Come on, everyone," Elizabeth cut in, looking angrily at Lila. "Let's *all* go."

Together, they ran across the playground to talk to the principal.

"Mrs. Armstrong," Elizabeth began. "We want to give Mrs. Becker wedding presents, but we don't know what to get."

The principal smiled. "Let me think," she began. "Maybe instead of each of you getting Mrs. Becker separate wedding presents, the whole class could get just one special gift that would be from all of you."

"That's a great idea!" Jessica said.

"How much money should we each give?" Todd asked.

Mrs. Armstrong thought for a moment. "I think two dollars sounds about right."

Elizabeth gulped. She had spent almost all her allowance on some new books. All she had left was thirty-five cents.

"My father would give me much more than that," Lila said with her chin in the air. "All I have to do is ask him."

"I'm going to use my *own* money," Todd said. "That'll make it extra special."

"Me, too," said Winston. Elizabeth agreed with Todd and Winston. If she asked her parents for two dollars, it wouldn't be a present from *her*. But that meant she would have to earn the money all by herself.

How was she going to do that?

CHAPTER 2

Lemonade for Sale!

Jessica took a jump rope out of her school bag when she got off the bus. "Carry my books, Liz," she said to her sister. And before Elizabeth could answer, Jessica began to skip rope down the sidewalk.

Elizabeth walked beside her, carrying both book bags. "Let's earn the money for Mrs. Becker's present," she said. "Don't you think that's a good idea?"

Jessica wrinkled her nose. "Let's just ask Mom and Dad for our share. That's what Lila's doing. Besides, we have to give four dollars, not two."

"But it would be a better present if we used our own money," Elizabeth said. The twins walked down their front walk. Elizabeth opened the front door of their house. Jessica dropped her jump rope on the steps and followed Elizabeth inside. She only had seven cents saved, and four dollars sounded like so much money. They'd never earn that much. And besides, Lila would tease her about it.

"Hi, girls." Mrs. Wakefield greeted them. She was in the kitchen, drawing on graph paper. It was part of her homework assignment for decorating class. "How was school today?"

"Fine, Mom," Elizabeth answered. She got out two glasses, while Jessica took a pitcher of lemonade out of the refrigerator. "Mom, we each want to earn two dollars to help buy Mrs. Becker's wedding present."

9

"I think that's a wonderful idea!" their mother said, smiling at them. Since Jessica was closer, Mrs. Wakefield gave her a big kiss. "You're both so generous!"

Jessica smiled back. She decided Elizabeth was right. "It'll be special that way," she said. "But how can we earn four dollars?" she asked, taking a sip of her lemonade.

Mrs. Wakefield looked thoughtful. Then she pointed to Jessica's glass. "Does that give you any ideas?"

Jessica looked at Elizabeth. Elizabeth smiled. "A lemonade stand?" she asked.

"Yes!" Jessica said. "That sounds like fun!"

"We can put a table out on the sidewalk and sell lemonade tomorrow," Elizabeth said eagerly. "Do we have any paper cups?"

Jessica ran to the cupboard where they kept paper napkins and picnic supplies.

"There's a whole bunch here!" she said, pulling out a tower of colorful cups.

"How much should we sell it for?" Elizabeth went on. "If we charge ten cents a cup, we have to sell . . ." She divided ten into four dollars, using a piece of Mrs. Wakefield's graph paper. "Forty cups?"

"Very good, Elizabeth," Mrs. Wakefield said. "That's right."

Jessica frowned. "Forty cups? That's a lot!"

"Don't worry, Jess," Elizabeth said. "We'll do it." But forty cups sounded like a lot to her too.

The next day was Saturday. After breakfast Jessica carried a full pitcher of lemonade outside. It was heavy, and the lemonade kept splashing over the edge.

"I spilled it all over me!" Jessica said, put-

11

ting the pitcher down on the table with a thump. "I have to wash my hands."

Elizabeth was busy finishing their signs: FRESH LEMONADE. 10 CENTS A CUP! She gave Jessica a napkin. "You can use this."

"My hands are all sticky," Jessica grumbled, sitting down in the chair next to Elizabeth. "Plus we're missing the best TV shows."

Elizabeth taped the sign carefully to the edge of the table. "We can watch next week."

Mr. Wakefield came outside with his camera in his hand. "I want to take a picture of my favorite businesswomen," he announced.

Jessica's face brightened. "Pictures!" she said, running around to the front of the table. "Does the sign show, Daddy?" she asked. Elizabeth stood next to her.

"Perfect!" Mr. Wakefield said from behind

the camera. "Say *pretty please pass the cheese*."

"Pretty please pass the cheese!" Jessica and Elizabeth shouted at the same time.

The camera clicked, and Mr. Wakefield smiled. "Great. Now go get 'em, girls! Sell that lemonade." He went back inside.

"I hope it's hot today," Elizabeth said as they sat down behind the table again. "Then people will be thirsty."

"It's always hot in California," Jessica reminded her. She poured herself a cup of lemonade. "I'm thirsty already." She gulped down her drink and poured some more.

Elizabeth laughed. "Don't drink it all!"

"I won't." Jessica looked up and down the sidewalk. "How come no one is coming?"

"They will," Elizabeth said confidently. "It's still early."

13

Jessica sipped her lemonade. "This is boring."

"Jessica!" Elizabeth gave her sister a pretend punch on the arm. "We only started two minutes ago!"

"I know, but we haven't made a single penny so far," Jessica pointed out.

Elizabeth smiled. "We will. You'll see."

Jessica shrugged and slumped down in her chair. She thought there were better things to do than spend all day trying to sell forty cups of lemonade.

CHAPTER 3

A Helping Hand

"Jess!" Elizabeth said suddenly. She pointed down the street. "Customers!" she said excitedly. Two teenage girls were walking toward them.

"Ask them if they're thirsty," Jessica said.

"OK." Elizabeth stood up and waved. "Lemonade! Ten cents a cup!" she called out.

The girls came closer. "Ten cents?" a girl with long brown hair asked. "I'll have a cup."

"Me, too," said her friend.

The girls each gave Jessica a dime, and Elizabeth poured out two cups.

FRESH
LEMONADE
10¢ A CUP

"Thanks," the girls said, drinking quickly and handing back the cups.

"You're welcome!" Elizabeth said brightly. "Look!" she told Jessica in a happy voice. She stacked the two dimes together. "Twenty cents already!"

"I wish they had asked for seconds," Jessica said after the girls walked away. "Then we would have *forty* cents."

Elizabeth threw the dirty cups into the garbage pail she had brought outside. "We'll make it. You'll see."

"Look!" Jessica said. "Here come Lila and Ellen! Hi!" she yelled.

Lila was riding her new bike, and Ellen Riteman was right behind her. They stopped by the lemonade stand.

"What are you doing?" Lila asked in surprise.

"We're selling lemonade," Elizabeth told

17

them. "We're earning money for Mrs. Becker's present."

"You have to *earn* the money?" Lila asked. She smiled at Jessica. "That's too bad. My father gave me the two dollars last night. Now Ellen and I are going to the park."

"That's right," Ellen added. "My mom is meeting us there. She's going to buy us ice cream."

Jessica felt left out. "I wish I could go," she muttered.

Elizabeth stared at her twin. "But . . ."

"Why can't you come, Jessica?" Lila asked. "I mean, do you *both* have to stay here to sell lemonade?"

"Well . . ." Jessica began. She looked hopefully at Elizabeth. "Do you mind if I go to the park for a while, Liz?" she asked.

Elizabeth looked down at the ground. She

18

felt angry, but she didn't want to tell her sister. "No," she said in a quiet voice.

"Great!" Jessica said. "You're the best, Liz! I'll get my bicycle, and I'll be right back," she said, running to the garage.

"Do you want some lemonade?" Elizabeth asked her sister's friends.

"No, thanks," Ellen said. Lila didn't answer. A minute later, Jessica pedaled down the driveway.

"I'm ready," she told Lila and Ellen. She smiled at Elizabeth. "Thanks, Liz. Just tell Mom where I went, OK?"

Jessica, Lila, and Ellen rode off toward the park. It seemed very quiet and lonely when they were gone. Elizabeth sat in her chair again and waited for people to come by.

"Hi, Elizabeth," called a voice.

Elizabeth looked up. Todd Wilkins was

walking toward her. He lived a few blocks away. "Hi, Todd," she said softly.

"What's wrong?" He looked at the FRESH LEMONADE sign. "Are you making money for Mrs. Becker's wedding present?"

Elizabeth nodded and tried to look cheerful. "Yes, but Jessica went to the park with Lila and Ellen. So I'm doing it by myself."

"That's too bad," Todd said. He tossed a softball and caught it in his mitt. "I'm helping my dad clean our car and straighten out the garage tomorrow. That's how I'm earning the money. Hey, here comes a car. Lemonade! Ten cents!" he yelled as the car got closer.

The car stopped, and a woman rolled down the window. "That sounds refreshing. We'll take three cups!"

Elizabeth smiled. "Coming right up," she said. She looked at Todd. "Thanks," she whispered.

"Want me to stay and help?" he asked, tossing his softball again. He didn't look at her.

Elizabeth nodded shyly. "If you want to."

More and more people came down the street on bikes, or in cars, or on foot. Elizabeth and Todd sold so many cups of lemonade that Elizabeth had to run inside three times to refill the pitcher. By noon, all the lemonade was gone, and Elizabeth had three dollars!

"Thanks, Todd," Elizabeth said, gathering up the coins.

He shrugged. "That's okay. See you in school."

Elizabeth smiled as he walked away. It did feel good to earn the money herself. She couldn't wait to tell Jessica they only needed one more dollar for their share of Mrs. Becker's wedding present.

CHAPTER 4

A New Bracelet

On Monday, Jessica and Elizabeth and some of their friends were gathered around Ken Matthews's desk before class started. They were talking about the wedding present.

"Is everybody chipping in?" Eva Simpson asked. She was one of the newer students in class but already had many friends.

"We told everyone about the two dollars," Winston said. "Everyone thinks it's a great idea."

Jessica was glad she and Elizabeth already had three dollars. Half of it was hers, so that meant she had one dollar and fifty cents. It also meant she only needed fifty cents more.

"We'll be able to get a really nice present," Caroline Pearce said. "Plus I'm very good at wrapping packages and tying bows."

Just then Mrs. Becker walked into the room.

"Shh. We have to speak quietly now," Elizabeth said in a whisper. She looked over her shoulder at Mrs. Becker. Their teacher sat at her desk and began to cut an article out of a newspaper. "Somebody has to keep the money. Who can we give it to?"

Ken leaned over his desk and spoke quietly. "Since it's a lot of money, it should be someone good at math."

All at once, everybody turned to look at Andy Franklin who sat in the front row. "Andy!" Lila called out.

Andy turned around in surprise, as if he couldn't believe Lila was speaking to him.

"Andy, come here!" Lila ordered.

Slowly Andy stood up and walked toward Lila. "What is it?"

"We want you to keep all the money we collect for Mrs. Becker's present," Elizabeth explained. "Will you?"

Andy's face turned pink. "O—OK," he stammered.

Lila rolled her eyes and whispered to Jessica, "He is so weird, isn't he?"

"I know what you mean," Jessica answered. She looked at Lila's hand. "Did you get a new bracelet?" she asked.

Lila held up her wrist. "Yes. It glows in the dark," she said proudly. "I got it at the mall. Do you like it?"

Jessica shrugged one shoulder. She didn't want Lila to think she was interested, but

Jessica wished she could have one, or even two bracelets. That way she'd have one more than Lila. Jessica thought a pink one would look nice in the dark.

"My mother is taking me shopping after school," Lila went on, as they walked to their desks. "Do you want to come?"

"I have to go home first and ask my mother," Jessica said.

"Maybe you can buy something, too," Lila said, taking a brand new strawberry-shaped eraser out of her desk. Lila always had new, pretty things, and she always showed them off.

Jessica frowned. Lila thought she was better than everyone else because she always had money to buy things. *But she isn't the only one,* Jessica thought. She thought about her share of the three dollars. She didn't want to spend it, but if she had the money with her, maybe then Lila wouldn't act so stuck up.

Jessica looked across the aisle at her sister. Elizabeth was going to Amy Sutton's house after school. Maybe Jessica could even take the whole three dollars. That would really show Lila. Elizabeth would never know she had borrowed it just for a little while.

I won't use it, Jessica told herself firmly.

Then she glanced at Lila's new glow-in-the-dark bracelet.

But I do wish I had one of those, she thought.

CHAPTER 5

The Perfect Gift

Elizabeth was using the pencil sharpener during art class. While she was turning the crank, someone tapped her on the shoulder.

"Elizabeth?" said a shy voice.

When Elizabeth turned around, she saw Lois Waller standing in front of her. "Hi, Lois."

Lois was holding a catalog from the Sweet Valley gift shop against her chest. "I found something really nice," she whispered. "I want to know what you think." She opened the catalog to a page she had folded over.

Elizabeth looked at the page Lois showed her. She saw a picture of a glass paperweight in the shape of an apple. The price was thirty-eight dollars and ninety-five cents.

"That is pretty," Elizabeth said. Then she gasped and stared at Lois. "You mean, this would be Mrs. Becker's wedding present?"

Lois smiled and nodded. Her cheeks were turning pink with excitement. "Yes. We'll have just enough money. There are twenty kids in our class. Twenty times two dollars equals forty dollars, right?"

"Right," Elizabeth whispered. "Let's pass this around to show everyone. But we can't let Mrs. You-Know-Who see it!"

Giggling, Lois folded the catalog so that only the paperweight showed. Then Elizabeth circled it with her pencil and wrote: IF YOU WANT TO PICK THIS FOR MRS. BECKER'S WEDDING PRESENT, TELL LOIS OR ELIZABETH.

"Cross off my name," Lois whispered. "Just put yours on there."

"But it's your idea," Elizabeth said. "Your name should be there, too."

Lois shook her head. "People don't like me as much as they like you. They might not like the idea if they knew it came from me," she said.

"Oh, Lois," Elizabeth said. "That's silly. And it's not true. But I'll take your name off if you want me to."

Elizabeth erased Lois's name. Then the two girls walked back to the art tables. Mrs. Becker was on the other side of the room, helping Sandra Ferris with her art project. The class was making collages with different-shaped pasta noodles.

"Jessica." Elizabeth tapped her sister on the shoulder. She handed Jessica the catalog while she kept her eyes on Mrs. Becker. If

Mrs. Becker saw what they were doing, it would spoil the surprise.

Jessica looked at the catalog and let out a soft *ooh*. "It's so pretty!" she whispered. She poked Ellen on the arm and passed the catalog to her.

Elizabeth smiled. She watched everyone at her table to see how they liked the paperweight. Each person who looked at the catalog nodded and started whispering. It looked like everyone thought it was a good choice for Mrs. Becker's present.

Eva was the last one at the table to see the catalog. She looked at Elizabeth and smiled. Then she tiptoed to the next table and handed the catalog to Ken.

Soon, everyone was whispering and smiling and trying to pass the catalog around without Mrs. Becker seeing. Elizabeth bit her lower lip and looked at the teacher. Mrs.

Becker seemed to be watching what they were doing but she didn't say anything. She just smiled and went to her desk.

"Someone must be passing around a very funny joke," she said.

Suddenly, the whole class was silent. Elizabeth's heart went *thud-thump* inside her chest. She was afraid she might burst out laughing at any moment. Jessica sat with both hands clamped over her mouth, and her eyes sparkled.

"Well, if no one wants to tell me," Mrs. Becker sighed, "I guess I'll never know."

Elizabeth snuck a glance at her sister. She wanted to smile, but she didn't dare. One of the boys snickered.

"It's time to start cleaning up," Mrs. Becker said. She was smiling. "Let's get these art supplies put away."

Instantly, the class began rushing around

to clean up. Winston bumped into Ken and spilled a whole jar of wheel-shaped macaronis on the floor. Elizabeth moved her collage to the windowsill to dry, and Jessica followed her.

"She knows something's going on!" Jessica whispered breathlessly. "That was close."

Elizabeth looked over at Mrs. Becker. "Do you think she knows what we're planning? I hope she doesn't see the catalog."

"She won't." Jessica shook her head. "The present is going to be a total surprise for her. I can't wait!"

Elizabeth let her breath out in a happy sigh. "Me neither. I'm glad we're all buying the present together," she said. "Mrs. Becker's going to love it."

"I know," Jessica agreed. "This will be the best present she ever got."

CHAPTER 6

Carried Away

When Jessica got home from school, Mrs. Wakefield gave her permission to go shopping with Lila. Jessica ran to the phone to call Lila.

"Great," said Lila. "We'll pick you up in twenty minutes."

Jessica hung up the telephone and went to her room. On the night table between her bed and Elizabeth's bed was a pile of quarters, dimes, and nickels. It was the three dollars from the lemonade stand.

More than anything, Jessica wanted to show Lila she had as much spending money as Lila did. One at a time, Jessica picked up enough coins to make one dollar and fifty cents. That was her share. She found her pink satin purse, unzipped it, and put the change inside.

The coins made a nice jingling sound when Jessica picked up the purse. They would jingle even more with the rest of the coins inside, she decided. So she scooped Elizabeth's share of the money into her purse. Now Lila wouldn't act so stuck up, she thought happily. She shook her purse and the coins went *klinkachink*.

"Jessica!" Mrs. Wakefield called. "Lila and Mrs. Fowler are here!"

Jessica felt a tiny bit bad about having all the money. But she wasn't going to *spend* it, she reminded herself. She just wanted to show it to Lila. She held her purse tight and ran downstairs.

"Hi," she said, getting into the back seat of the Fowlers' car.

With wide eyes, Lila looked at Jessica's purse. "Are you going to buy something?"

"I don't know yet," Jessica said lightly. *"Maybe."*

"How much money do you have?" Lila asked.

Jessica lifted her chin and smiled. "Three dollars."

Lila didn't say anything. Jessica looked out the window and smiled to herself. Now Lila knew she wasn't the only one in their class who had spending money.

"Where do you want to go first, girls?" Mrs. Fowler asked when they pulled into the parking lot of the mall.

"Let's go to Heavenly Dolls!" Lila said quickly. "I want some new outfits for my Barbie." Then she looked at Jessica. "You

37

could get some new stuff for your dolls, too."

Jessica shrugged. "Maybe."

"Do you want to see my bracelet glow in the dark?" Lila asked, holding out her arm.

"But it's not dark yet," Jessica pointed out.

Lila gave her a that's-what-you-think smile. "Watch."

She put her jacket over her wrist. "You can see it like this," she said.

Jessica leaned close to look. The bracelet did glow, even though it wasn't very dark.

"That's neat," Jessica said, trying not to sound too jealous.

"I got it at the store next to Heavenly Dolls," Lila said. "Why don't you get one, too? They only cost one dollar and forty cents."

Jessica gulped. She knew she wasn't supposed to spend the money. But a dollar and fifty cents of it was hers.

Jessica shook her head. "I don't know," she said. "I might not buy anything."

Jessica, Lila, and Mrs. Fowler walked into the mall. Their first stop was the doll store. Lila's mother bought the tennis dress, the evening gown, and the rock-star outfit Lila picked out for her doll.

"Those are really nice," Jessica said, wishing the outfits could be for her doll. She played with the zipper on her purse. Then she opened it and looked inside. All the quarters and dimes and nickels were there, shiny and bright.

"Come on," Lila said. "Let's look at the bracelets. They come in a lot of different colors."

Jessica followed her friend to the store

next door. On the counter was a glass case filled with glow-in-the-dark bracelets. There were pink ones, blue ones, yellow ones—almost every color of the rainbow. Jessica chose a pink one and tried it on.

"That looks nice on you," Lila said.

"I really like it," Jessica agreed. She tried on a blue one, too. "They look good together."

"Get them both!" Lila suggested. "Go on!"

Jessica bit her lip. Then she nodded. "OK," she whispered. "I will."

CHAPTER 7

"Where's the Money?"

Elizabeth came home from Amy's house just before dinnertime. She ran upstairs to put her schoolbooks on her desk.

"Hi, Jessica," she called.

Jessica was sitting on her bed playing with her stuffed animals. She put one arm behind her when Elizabeth entered the room. "Oh, hi," she said quietly.

"What's wrong with your arm?" Elizabeth asked, looking at Jessica.

"What do you mean?" Jessica said in a squeaky voice.

Elizabeth grinned. "You're holding it in a funny way."

"No, I'm not," Jessica said.

"Do you have something in your hand?" Elizabeth asked.

Jessica shook her head from side to side. "No."

Elizabeth knew her sister was hiding something. "Come on," she teased. "What is it?" Elizabeth ran to the bed and tried to look behind Jessica's back.

"Hey," Jessica said, flopping onto her back with her arm underneath her. "Quit it!"

Elizabeth sat down next to her sister. "But what is it?"

Jessica sat up again. "Nothing," she said with a shrug.

Quickly, Elizabeth leaned over and looked

at Jessica's hand. Her sister was wearing two bracelets like Lila's.

"When did you get those bracelets?" Elizabeth asked in surprise.

Jessica looked down at the floor. She twirled the bracelets around her wrist. "I don't know," she whispered.

"How could you not know?" Elizabeth asked. She was puzzled. Why was Jessica acting so mysterious?

Elizabeth looked over at the night table between the girls' beds, and her mouth dropped open.

"Jessica!" she gasped. "What happened to our money?"

"Ummm . . ." Jessica began. Her face was slowly turning red.

Elizabeth stared at her sister, and her face also became hot and red. "Did you spend

it? Did you buy those bracelets with our money?"

Instead of answering, Jessica burst into tears. "I didn't mean to!" she sobbed.

"You didn't spend it *all,* did you?" Elizabeth asked.

Jessica nodded and began to cry even harder.

Elizabeth felt so disappointed she couldn't think of anything to say. She felt like crying, too.

"Hey, now. What's the trouble, girls?" Mrs. Wakefield asked, walking into their room.

Elizabeth's chin began to tremble. She didn't like telling on her sister, but now she and Jessica wouldn't be able to help buy Mrs. Becker's wedding present. And she had worked so hard selling the lemonade, too. Elizabeth felt terrible.

"Mom," she sniffed. "Jessica spent our money! It's not fair!"

Jessica began to sob even harder.

Mrs. Wakefield frowned. "Now, Jessica, what exactly did you do?"

"I wasn't going to use it. I just wanted to take the money with me. And then I wanted the bracelets so much. I'm sorry!" Jessica choked out.

"But it was my money, too," Elizabeth pointed out. She couldn't believe her twin would do something like that. "Now I can't give my share for the present!"

"All right," their mother said. She sat down on Elizabeth's bed and thought for a minute. "This is what we'll do," she finally said. "Elizabeth, since you already worked so hard for your share, I'll give you your two dollars. But Jessica," she said in a stern

47

voice. "You are going to have to earn your two dollars."

Jessica took a deep breath and went on crying. "But Mommy . . ."

"No buts," Mrs. Wakefield said. "I was upset that you let Elizabeth do all the work on Saturday. So this is the only way to be fair. Now dry your eyes. It's time for dinner."

Jessica stood up and followed Mrs. Wakefield out of the room. But Elizabeth stayed where she was. She would still get to chip in her share for Mrs. Becker's present, but that didn't make her feel any better.

"How could Jessica do something like that?" she said out loud.

CHAPTER 8

Friends Again

"I have to clean out my half of the closet, empty the trash baskets, and rearrange the pots and pans?" Jessica whined. She and Elizabeth had just come home from school on Tuesday.

Mrs. Wakefield nodded. "That's right, Jessica. And I want those chores done before you even think about watching TV."

Jessica looked at her sister. Elizabeth ignored Jessica and continued to eat her chocolate-chip cookie.

"Does Liz get to watch TV?" Jessica asked grumpily.

Mrs. Wakefield frowned. "Elizabeth isn't the one who has to earn two dollars, Jessica."

"It's not fair," Jessica grumbled, opening the cupboard.

"What did you say?" her mother asked.

Jessica shook her head. "Nothing." She took the pots and pans, one by one, out of the cupboard and set them on the floor. *Clang. Bang. Clunk.*

Mrs. Wakefield walked into the living room. Elizabeth stayed in the kitchen. She began to read *Winnie-the-Pooh* and acted like Jessica wasn't in the same room.

"These pots are so heavy," Jessica said loudly. She glanced at her sister, but Elizabeth kept on reading.

"I didn't really mean to use the money," Jessica said sadly. She put a small pot inside a big pot and sniffled. "Lila made me."

Elizabeth turned a page.

Jessica sniffled again and wiped a tear off her cheek. She hated it when Elizabeth was angry at her. "I'm sorry, Lizzie. I really am."

The kitchen was very quiet. "Really?" Elizabeth asked.

Jessica nodded. "Really," she said, stacking more pots together. She put lids on some of the pans. It was going to take her all afternoon to do the chores. She sighed loudly.

Elizabeth turned around and looked at her. "That's the wrong one," she said, pointing to the lid Jessica was holding over a pot.

"Oh," Jessica picked out one that fit. Then she tried to find room for the pots in the cupboard. It was too crowded.

"Maybe you should put all the big pots back in first," Elizabeth suggested. She kneeled down next to Jessica. "Then there'll be room for the little ones."

Jessica smiled. "OK."

Together, they finished straightening up the cupboard. Next, Jessica found a large plastic trash bag. "I have to empty the waste-paper baskets, now," she said, looking hopefully at her sister. "Do you want to come with me?"

Elizabeth smiled and shrugged. "I guess."

"How come you're helping me?" Jessica asked.

"Well, Todd helped *me*," Elizabeth explained. "So I guess I can help you."

"Hooray!" Jessica laughed. "Come on." She ran into the den and picked up the trash basket by their father's desk. "Look at all the garbage Daddy makes!"

Elizabeth giggled and held the bag open while Jessica put the trash in. Then Elizabeth carried the bag over her shoulder. "Look! I'm Santa Claus!"

"With icky presents," Jessica said. Both girls laughed.

"Come on," Elizabeth said. "I'll race you upstairs."

Jessica screamed and ran behind Elizabeth. They sounded like a herd of elephants galloping up the stairs. When they had collected the trash from each of the bedrooms, it was time to clean out Jessica's half of the closet.

"This is going to take a long time," Elizabeth teased, opening the door to their large walk-in closet.

Jessica made a pretend-frightened face. "I might get lost in there."

"Come on," Elizabeth said with a laugh.

Jessica looked at the jumble of shoes and clothes on the floor and began tossing things over her shoulder. The farther back she went in the closet, the more her glow-in-the-dark bracelets showed.

"Lizzie, come here!" she whispered.

Elizabeth crawled in under the dresses with Jessica.

"You know what?" Jessica said, taking off the blue bracelet. "You're the best sister in the whole world. I want you to have this one."

Elizabeth slipped the bracelet on and waved her hand around. The bracelet made blue zigzags in the dark. "Thanks, Jess," she said.

Jessica smiled. "Are we best friends again?" she asked.

"Yes," Elizabeth answered.

The twins grinned at each other as their bracelets glowed in the dark.

CHAPTER 9

Forty Dollars

At recess on Wednesday, Elizabeth and Jessica found Andy on the swings. "Here's my two dollars," Elizabeth said.

"And here's mine," Jessica added. They each handed Andy their money.

Andy flattened out the dollar bills. "OK. Now everyone has turned in their money," he said.

"Great!" Elizabeth said. She squeezed Jessica's hand. "Now we can get Mrs. Becker's present!"

Lila, Todd, Ellen, and Winston walked over. "Mrs. Armstrong is over at the slide.

She's scolding Charlie and Jerry again," Lila said.

"Shh! Quiet, everyone!" Jessica said in a loud whisper. She pointed to Mrs. Becker, who was standing by the jungle gym. "We've got all the money," Jessica told them. "Let's tell Mrs. Armstrong."

Todd and Winston started running, but Elizabeth shouted. "Wait! Where's Lois?"

"Who wants old crybaby Lois?" Winston said.

Elizabeth frowned at him. "It was Lois's idea to get the paperweight," she told them. "She should come, too."

No one said anything. Elizabeth spotted Lois watching two girls on the seesaw.

"Over here, Lois!" Elizabeth called waving her arms.

Lois's eyes widened, and she hurried over.

"Do you still have the catalog?" Elizabeth asked.

Lois nodded up and down.

"Then what are we waiting for?" Lila said. "Let's go!"

Elizabeth grabbed Jessica's hand, and the group raced across the playground.

"Mrs. Armstrong!" Jessica shouted while they ran.

The principal turned around. She looked a bit startled to see so many kids running toward her.

"What's wrong?" she said quickly.

Lila was panting. She nudged Lois. "Show her," she said.

Lois's cheeks turned pink. She took the catalog from her pocket and unfolded it. She held it out for Mrs. Armstrong to see.

"We picked this for Mrs. Becker," Elizabeth explained. She pointed to the picture of the paperweight. "We all agreed that's what we want to get for the class present. Do you think she'll like it?"

"Hmmm . . ." Mrs. Armstrong frowned looking closely at the picture. She nodded her head slowly and said, "Hmmm," again.

All eight boys and girls stared at their principal in suspense. Elizabeth crossed her fingers and then crossed her wrists for extra good luck. She hoped Mrs. Armstrong liked their choice.

"I think it's perfect," Mrs. Armstrong finally said. "She'll love it."

"Whew!" Todd gasped.

Lila poked Andy's arm. "Show her."

Andy pulled a handful of dollar bills out of his pants pocket. Some of them were crumpled into tiny balls. And some were folded up into neat squares. Mrs. Armstrong counted them as he handed them to her.

"This is only thirty five dollars," the principal said.

Andy nodded. "I know. The rest is in my other pocket," he explained. He kneeled down and emptied his pocket. A shower of quarters, nickels, and dimes came tinkling out onto the ground.

"Wow!" Lois exclaimed.

Elizabeth bent down to help Andy pick up the coins. "It's all here," Andy said. "I counted it five times!"

Mrs. Armstrong smiled. "You did a good job, Andy. But we'll need a few dollars more to pay the tax."

"Oh, no," everyone groaned at once.

"Don't worry. I'll pay the tax," Mrs. Armstrong added. "That will be my contri-

bution. And I'll bring the catalog with me to the gift shop so that I know just which paper-weight to buy."

"Yippee!" everyone shouted.

"Now all you have to do is wait for the wedding," the principal said.

"Yes!" Jessica laughed. She grabbed Elizabeth's hands and they jumped around in a circle.

Elizabeth giggled. It was going to be so exciting! She couldn't wait for Saturday.

CHAPTER 10

Wedding Bells

When Jessica woke up on Saturday morning, she sat straight up in bed. "Wake up, Lizzie!" she said, throwing her koala bear at the other bed.

Elizabeth rolled over and yawned. "Is it time for school?" she asked, still half asleep.

"No! It's time for Mrs. Becker's wedding!" Jessica giggled. "Wake up, sleepy-head!"

Elizabeth opened her eyes wide. "I almost forgot!"

After breakfast, Mrs. Wakefield came upstairs to help them brush their hair and get dressed.

"We want to wear our birthday dresses," Jessica announced. She opened the closet and walked inside.

"My goodness, it's so neat in there!" Mrs. Wakefield teased.

Jessica made a face. "Ha, ha," she said. Then she giggled. She was too excited to mind being teased.

She pulled her red long-sleeved dress with pink and green flowers off its hanger. Elizabeth had one just like it. They had bought them for their seventh birthday party.

"Now, sit still while I get your barrettes in," their mother said to Elizabeth.

"Do you think she'll like the present, Mom?" Elizabeth asked.

Mrs. Wakefield clipped a red barrette. "She'll love it. It sounds like a perfect present."

"It is," Jessica agreed. "When she opens it, she won't think about any other presents."

Mrs. Becker's wedding was taking place that morning in the backyard of a large house in Sweet Valley. Mr. Wakefield drove Elizabeth and Jessica there and told them he would come back to pick them up after the reception.

Jessica's eyes widened as they walked around to the back of the house. The garden was decorated with large white satin bows and bouquets of pink and yellow flowers. White chairs were lined up in neat rows, and a man in a tuxedo was showing people in party clothes to their seats. A woman in a light-blue dress was playing a violin.

"Look who's here!" Jessica whispered to Elizabeth.

Lila, Ellen, and Eva were already seated.

They turned around in their chairs and waved. "Sit with us!" Ellen called.

A woman frowned at Ellen and put her finger on her lips. Jessica and Elizabeth giggled as they walked very slowly down the aisle. Jessica ran the last few steps and sat down in a chair next to Lila.

"Isn't this exciting?" she gasped. "Look at all the people."

Lila shrugged. "I've been to lots of fancy weddings," she said.

"This is my first one," Eva said happily. "Isn't it fun? When will we see Mrs. Becker?"

Elizabeth looked over her shoulder. "I don't know. Here come some more kids from class!"

Todd, Winston, and Ken were walking down the aisle. They all looked very neatly dressed, except one piece of Winston's hair stuck up in back.

"I never saw them wearing dress-up jackets before," Jessica whispered to Lila. Both girls giggled.

Soon, all the students from Mrs. Becker's class had arrived. They took up two whole rows. Everyone was whispering and giggling and squirming in the seats. A minister stood in front of the guests, and two men in gray suits stood facing him.

"That's Mr. Otis," Jessica whispered to her sister. She pointed to the handsome man on the left. The twins saw him whenever they went to the Sweet Valley Public Library. Mr. Otis was always very helpful. "Do you think he's nervous?"

Elizabeth nodded. "He must be." She looked around and then grabbed Jessica's arm. "Here she comes!"

At the same time, everyone stood up and turned around. The violinist began playing a beautiful, slow song, and Mrs. Becker began to walk down the aisle. She was wearing a lavender silk dress and held a bouquet of pink flowers. She smiled at everyone.

Jessica stood on tiptoe. "Doesn't she look pretty?"

Finally, Mrs. Becker reached the minister, and Mr. Otis took her hand and smiled at her.

"Yes," Elizabeth whispered back. "I'm glad she's marrying Mr. Otis."

Jessica and Elizabeth smiled at each other. Then they sat down and watched the ceremony. The minister had a nice voice, and he smiled a lot at Mrs. Becker and Mr. Otis. Then the other man held out two rings, and the bride and groom put them on.

"I now pronounce you husband and wife!" the minister said.

"Hooray!" the whole class cheered and began to stand up.

Mrs. Becker turned around and laughed. "Not yet, kids," she told them. Some of the grown-ups laughed, too.

Jessica put her hands to her mouth. "Oops," she whispered. "I guess they have to kiss."

Mr. Otis and the new Mrs. Otis kissed, then they held hands and walked back down the aisle. All of the wedding guests stood up and followed them to a yellow-and-white tent.

"When is she going to open the presents?" Jessica asked.

"We have to make sure she opens ours first," Lila said loudly.

Some of the other kids nodded. "Yeah," Charlie agreed. "Come on!"

They all ran to the tent and crowded around their teacher. "Open our present first!" Winston yelled.

68

"Please?" Elizabeth added.

Mrs. Otis laughed. "All right. I will." She turned and looked at the table piled with presents, each one wrapped in beautiful paper. "Which one is it?"

"It's small," Lila shouted.

"About this big," Todd suggested, holding up his hands.

"It's from all of us!" Ken chimed in.

Mrs. Armstrong picked up a small box wrapped in white paper with a pink bow. "This is from your class," she said, handing the present to Mrs. Otis.

Jessica held her breath while Mrs. Otis took off the paper and lifted the lid of the small box. There was a hush.

"Oh!" their teacher exclaimed. She wiped her eyes. "Oh!"

Jessica gulped and stared at Elizabeth. What was wrong?

"I love it!" Mrs. Otis said. She laughed and cried at the same time and held up the paperweight for everyone to see. "I wish I could hug you all at the same time!"

"I knew she would like it," Lois whispered. She was standing behind Jessica and Elizabeth, and she had a proud smile on her face.

"I would have picked that, too," Lila told everyone. "If I had seen the catalog first, I would have picked the paperweight."

Jessica looked at her sister, and they smiled at each other. Lila just *had* to show off!

"Now who wants some wedding cake?" their teacher asked.

While the rest of the class lined up for cake, Jessica and Elizabeth tapped Mrs. Otis on the arm.

"Yes, girls?" she asked them.

Elizabeth bit her lip. "We just want to

know," she began. "Will you still be our teacher?"

"Of course. You kids are the best in the world," Mrs. Otis said.

"And should we call you Mrs. Otis, now?" Jessica asked.

Mrs. Otis smiled. "Yes," she said. "I think that would be a good idea."

Elizabeth and Jessica were glad that Mrs. Becker was now Mrs. Otis and that she would still be their teacher.

The party was so much fun that no one wanted to leave. At three o'clock, Mr. Wakefield arrived to pick up the twins.

"It was really, really fun, Dad!" Jessica said, as they got into the car.

"Mrs. Becker, I mean Mrs. Otis, loved our present," Elizabeth added. "She was really surprised."

"That's wonderful," Mr. Wakefield said. "And now, I have a surprise for you."

Jessica bounced on her seat. "What?"

"Guess who's coming to visit?" he asked them.

Jessica and Elizabeth both shrugged. "Who?" Elizabeth wanted to know.

Mr. Wakefield smiled. "Grandma and Grandpa Wakefield!"

Jessica screamed. "Hooray!"

"*And* they want to take you girls on a trip."

"Where?" Elizabeth gasped.

Mr. Wakefield shook his head. "*That's* the surprise!"

Where will the Wakefield grandparents take Jessica and Elizabeth? Find out in Sweet Valley Kids #10, THE TWINS AND THE WILD WEST.

SWEET VALLEY KIDS

Jessica and Elizabeth have had lots of adventures in *Sweet Valley High* and *Sweet Valley Twins*...now read about the twins at age seven! You'll love all the fun that comes with being seven—birthday parties, playing dress-up, class projects, putting on puppet shows and plays, losing a tooth, setting up lemonade stands, caring for animals and much more! It's all part of SWEET VALLEY KIDS. Read them all!

☐ SURPRISE! SURPRISE! #1	15758-2	$2.75/$3.25
☐ RUNAWAY HAMSTER #2	15759-0	$2.75/$3.25
☐ THE TWINS' MYSTERY TEACHER # 3	15760-4	$2.75/$3.25
☐ ELIZABETH'S VALENTINE # 4	15761-2	$2.99/$3.50
☐ JESSICA'S CAT TRICK # 5	15768-X	$2.75/$3.25
☐ LILA'S SECRET # 6	15773-6	$2.75/$3.25
☐ JESSICA'S BIG MISTAKE # 7	15799-X	$2.75/$3.25
☐ JESSICA'S ZOO ADVENTURE # 8	15802-3	$2.75/$3.25
☐ ELIZABETH'S SUPER-SELLING LEMONADE #9	15807-4	$2.99/$3.50
☐ THE TWINS AND THE WILD WEST #10	15811-2	$2.75/$3.25
☐ CRYBABY LOIS #11	15818-X	$2.99/$3.50
☐ SWEET VALLEY TRICK OR TREAT #12	15825-2	$2.75/$3.25
☐ STARRING WINSTON EGBERT #13	15836-8	$2.75/$3.25
☐ JESSICA THE BABY-SITTER #14	15838-4	$2.75/$3.25
☐ FEARLESS ELIZABETH #15	15844-9	$2.75/$3.25
☐ JESSICA THE TV STAR #16	15850-3	$2.75/$3.25
☐ CAROLINE'S MYSTERY DOLLS #17	15870-8	$2.75/$3.25
☐ BOSSY STEVEN #18	15881-3	$2.75/$3.25
☐ JESSICA AND THE JUMBO FISH #19	15936-4	$2.99/$3.50
☐ THE TWINS GO TO THE HOSPITAL #20	15912-7	$2.99/$3.50
☐ THE CASE OF THE SECRET SANTA (SVK Super Snooper #1)	15860-0	$2.95/$3.50
☐ THE CASE OF THE MAGIC CHRISTMAS BELL (SVK Super Snooper #2)	15964-X	$2.99/$3.50

A BANTAM SKYLARK BOOK

FRANCINE PASCAL'S

SWEET VALLEY
Twins AND FRIENDS®

Buy them at your local bookstore or use this handy page for ordering:

Bantam Books, Dept. SVT3, 2451 S. Wolf Road, Des Plaines, IL 60018

Please send me the items I have checked above. I am enclosing $_____
(please add $2.50 to cover postage and handling). Send check or money
order, no cash or C.O.D.s please.

Mr/Ms _____

Address _____

City/State _____ Zip_____

SVT3-4/93

Please allow four to six weeks for delivery.
Prices and availability subject to change without notice.